Happy Easter, Hello Kitty®

By Rebecca Gómez
Illustrated by Sachiho Hino

W9-CGM-238

SCHOLASTIC INC.

New York Toronto London Auckland
Sydney Mexico City New Delhi Hong Kong

ISBN 978-0-545-45902-0

Printed in the U.S.A.   40
This edition first printing, March 2012

Hello Kitty invited her friends home after school.

They wanted to decorate Easter eggs together.

Hello Kitty and Mimmy were having an Easter
egg hunt the next day.

Fifi and Tracy were helping them color eggs today.

It was going to be so much fun!

Tracy wanted to color lots of eggs.

Hello Kitty wanted to find plenty of eggs.

Mama and Papa were going to hide all the
eggs.

Hello Kitty and her friends were going to be given Easter baskets.

When all the eggs were hidden, Mama would let everyone know when the hunt can begin.

Toot! Toot! The bus beeped its horn.
It was at Hello Kitty and Mimmy's stop.

Hello Kitty was excited for the fun to begin.

Mama met them at the door.

She invited them in for cookies.

They thanked Mrs. White.

The cookies were delicious.

Mama got out everything they needed to make Easter eggs.

Mimmy and Hello Kitty helped Mama boil
the eggs last night.

Now Mama placed the eggs in a big bowl.

Then she put out crayons, markers, scissors, stickers, and glue.

Fifi and Hello Kitty helped Mama mix colors in small bowls.

They mixed blue, yellow, and red.

Mama explained how to mix these colors to make other colors.

Fifi wanted to make simple and fancy eggs.

Mimmy liked fancy eggs.

The four friends colored, dipped, and stickered eggs all afternoon.

Tracy showed his egg first.

Everyone laughed at how silly it looked.

Fifi showed hers next.

Hello Kitty thought it looked just like a rainbow.

Hello Kitty made her egg look like a rabbit.

Then Mimmy showed hers.

It was the most beautiful egg they had ever seen!

Fifi thought it was too pretty to hide.

Mimmy smiled.

The next day, Mama and Papa hid the eggs all around the yard.
Everyone came to Hello Kitty's house for the hunt.

Mama told everyone that they can start the egg
hunt. They found lots of eggs.
But poor Tracy didn't find any!

Hello Kitty saw that Tracy's basket was empty.
Mimmy saw that Tracy was sad.

Hello Kitty and Mimmy had a great idea to surprise Tracy.

Suddenly, Tracy found Mimmy's sparkly, beautiful Easter egg!